# My First Book

WRITTEN BY JANE BELK MONCURE • ILLUSTRATED BY REBECCA THORNBURGH

**The Child's World®**
childsworld.com

Published by The Child's World®
1980 Lookout Drive • Mankato, MN 56003-1705
800-599-READ • www.childsworld.com

ISBN HARDCOVER: 9781503823020
ISBN PAPERBACK: 9781503831247
LCCN: 2017960244

Printed in the United States of America
PA02371

## A NOTE TO PARENTS AND EDUCATORS:

Magic moon machines and five fat frogs are just a few of the fun things you can share with children by reading books with them. Reading aloud helps children in so many ways! It introduces them to new words, motivates them to develop their own reading skills, and expands their attention span and listening abilities. So it's important to find time each day to share a book or two . . . or three!

As you read with young children, you can help develop their understanding of how print works by talking about the parts of the book—the cover, the title, the illustrations, and the words that tell the story. As you read, use your finger to point to each word, modeling a gentle sweep from left to right.

Simple word games help develop important prereading skills, including an understanding of rhyme and alliteration (when words share the same beginning sound, such as "six" and "sand"). Try playing with words from a book you've just shared: "What other words start with the same sound as moon?" "Cat and hat, do those words rhyme?" The possibilities are endless—and so are the rewards!

# My First Book

# eyes

# nose

# mouth

hair

feet

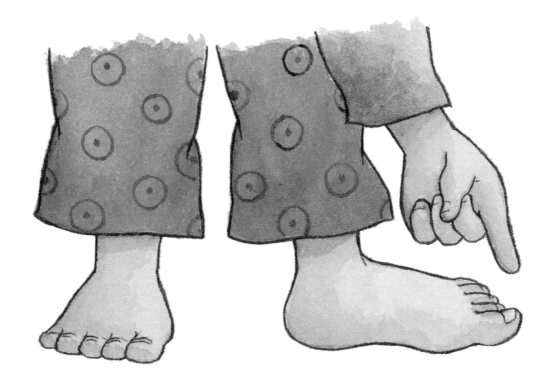

toes

# Mommy

# Daddy

hug

# friends

# balloons

hats

pajamas

# bed

cup

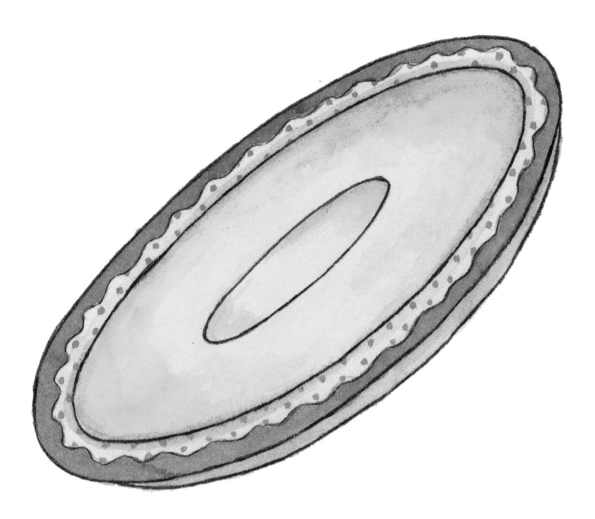

plate

apple

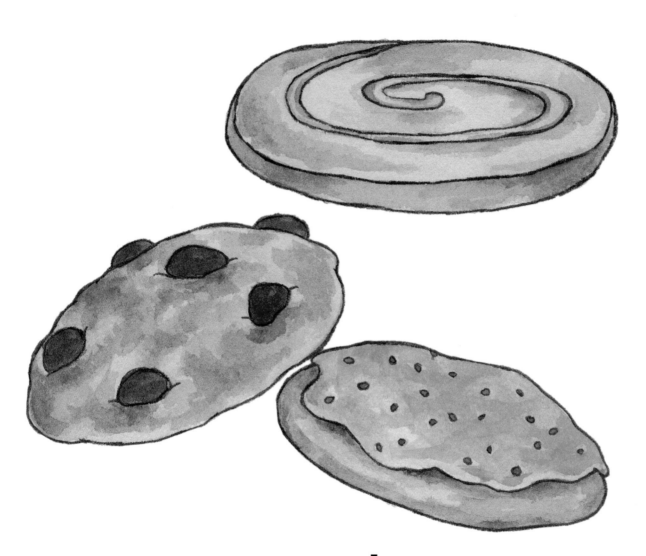

cookies

ball

# wagon

bear

doll

bunny

# blocks

# box

# I will fill my box.

# More to Do!

You learned many new words in this book. The words are about things you see every day. They are all about you! You can make a big picture of you. Here is what you will need:

## What you need:
- a very big piece of paper
- markers or crayons

## Directions:
Lie down on the paper. Have someone trace around you. It might tickle! Now it is time to fill in the details. Draw your eyes, nose, mouth, ears, and hair. Do you have freckles? Do you have pierced ears? Be sure to remember everything. Now draw some clothes. Maybe you will want to draw your favorite pajamas or your best sweater. How many words from the book can you use in your picture?

# About the Author

Best-selling author Jane Belk Moncure (1926–2013) wrote more than 300 books throughout her teaching and writing career. After earning a master's degree in early childhood education from Columbia University, she became one of the pioneers in that field. In 1956, she helped form the Virginia Association for Early Childhood Education, which established the first statewide standards for teachers of young children.

Inspired by her work in the classroom, Mrs. Moncure's books became standards in primary education, and her name was recognized across the country. Her success was reflected not only in her books' popularity with parents, children, and educators, but also by numerous awards, including the 1984 C. S. Lewis Gold Medal Award.

# About the Illustrator

Rebecca Thornburgh lives in a pleasantly spooky old house in Philadelphia. If she's not at her drawing table, she's reading—or singing with her band, called Reckless Amateurs. Rebecca has one husband, two daughters, and two silly dogs.